This book belongs to

_____

Disney's 102 DALMATIANS

A READ-ALOUD STORYBOOK

Adapted by Zoe Benjamin

MOUSE WORKS™

Find us at www.disneybooks.com for more Mouse Works fun!

102 Dalmatians is based on the book *The Hundred and One Dalmatians* by Dodie Smith, published by The Viking Press.

Printed in the United States of America.

ISBN 0-7364-0195-4

Cruella on the Loose

Cruella De Vil was free from prison. She was a changed woman. Now she was kind to all animals—even dogs.

The judge warned Cruella that if she ever returned to her puppynapping ways, he would take away her freedom—and her fortune.

Cruella's loyal assistant, Alonso, picked her up from prison. He brought her a gift. The frightened, hairless puppy growled at Cruella.

"Look, he's smiling at me," cooed Cruella. She named her new dog Fluffy.

Kevin Shepherd ran the Second Chance Dog Shelter. He loved dogs. He played tug-of-war with Drooler while the other dogs watched.

Waddlesworth, a macaw who thought he was a dog, cheered them on.

But Second Chance was in trouble. Kevin did not have the rent money.

His landlord told him, "You and your mangy pack

are out of here tomorrow!"

"You can't turn all these dogs loose in the city," protested Kevin. But his landlord did not care.

The landlord returned the next day to kick out Kevin and the dogs.

But Cruella had heard about Kevin's misfortune. She decided to buy the shelter!

Chloe Simon was in charge of Cruella's probation. She watched over Cruella to make sure she stayed out of trouble.

"I don't trust anyone who knowingly puts Cruella
De Vil anywhere near dogs!" Chloe told Kevin.

Chloe kept a close eye on Cruella. She saw Cruella transform Second Chance into an animal palace. Cruella even gave the dogs new hairstyles and bubble baths!

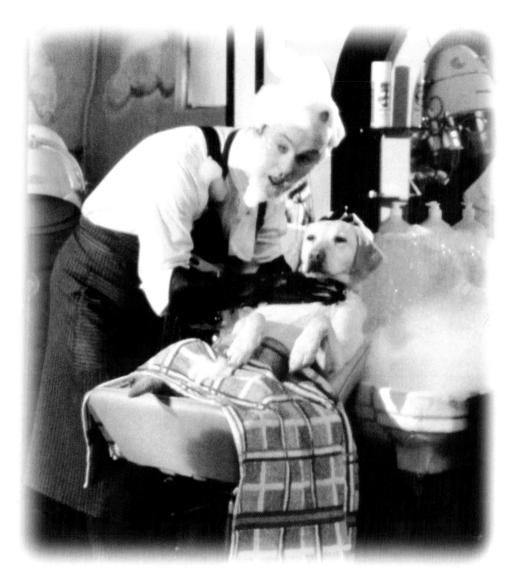

Chloe had dogs of her own—Dipstick, Dottie, and their puppies. One day she brought them to work. Agnes, Chloe's boss, met the dogs for the first time. "So you're Domino," she said to the pup with the domino on his collar. "Little Dipper, your tail is just like Daddy's. I know you, Oddball, because you don't have any—"

"Shh!" interrupted Chloe. She knew Oddball felt left out because she hadn't gotten her spots.

Then Cruella came in for her visit. While Chloe was talking to her, the puppies quickly got into trouble. They wound up out on the window ledge! Cruella spotted the endangered pups, and Chloe rescued them.

But something was happening to Cruella. . . .

Outside Chloe's open window, Big Ben was chiming loudly. The noise had a strange effect on Cruella. Her hair sprang up wildly. Everywhere she looked she saw spots. She ran from Chloe's office. The cruel was returning to Cruella!

Cruel Cruella

Cruella quickly decided that she had to make the Dalmatian puppy coat that she had designed years earlier.

She knew just the furrier to help her—Jean Pierre LePelt. She went to his fur fashion show and enlisted his help.

Meanwhile, Chloe and Kevin happened to meet up in the park with all their pets. Everyone was enjoying a puppet show when Oddball climbed up on the stage! She wanted to help a spotted puppet.

Oddball ran off the stage and tumbled onto a balloon seller. Tangled up in balloon strings, Oddball began floating away!

Kevin begged Waddlesworth to rescue Oddball. But
when Waddlesworth hopped from Kevin's hand, he fell to
the ground. "Dogs can't fly! Can't fly!" he squawked sadly.

27

Kevin ran after Oddball and the balloons. He climbed on top of the puppet theater. He jumped for the balloon strings . . . and caught them!

He and Oddball landed safely on a playground slide. Chloe was so happy to have the little pup back.

On the other side of town, Cruella and LePelt
worked on a new design for a spotted puppy coat.
Cruella wanted more puppies than ever before.

"We need one hundred and two," she said. "This time I want a *hooded* spotted puppy coat."

Cruella had Alonso steal dozens of Dalmatian puppies. Her assistant was badly bruised and bitten when he returned to her.

She soon had a new mission for him: leave a few of
the stolen pups at Second Chance. She wanted to
make sure someone else took the blame for her crime.

The next morning, police officers showed up at Kevin's door. They had a phone tip about some stolen Dalmatian pups.

The police found the pups at Second Chance.

"I'm being set up!" protested Kevin. "Why would I steal Dalmatians?"

Chloe and Cruella arrived at Second Chance.
"If I'm caught stealing puppies, my fortune goes to
him," Cruella said, pointing at Kevin. "Would that be

a motive?" The police took Kevin and his animals to jail. Chloe was very upset, and Cruella pretended she felt bad, too.

Get Those Puppies!

Cruella invited Chloe and Dipstick to a fancy party at her house. "You need a distraction," she told Chloe.

But the party was just another part of Cruella's heartless plan. She wanted to dognap Chloe's Dalmatian puppies!

As the guests and their dogs ate, Dipstick heard a tiny bark. He saw Fluffy, Cruella's hairless dog, signaling to him. He and Chloe followed Fluffy out of the room.

Wanting to help, Fluffy led Dipstick and Chloe to Cruella's fur room. Chloe gasped when she saw the design for the Dalmatian puppy coat!

"Surprise!" cackled Cruella behind them. She locked the door—but not before Dipstick escaped.

Dipstick raced home to save his family. Cruella had sent LePelt to dognap the puppies, but they gave him quite a fight. Oddball managed to start the Twilight Bark— soon, dogs all over London were barking the news about the puppynapping.

Dipstick arrived home just after LePelt had finally captured Dottie and the puppies. With a giant leap, Dipstick landed in the back of LePelt's truck.

At the jail, Kevin's dogs heard the Twilight Bark. Waddlesworth translated the barks for Kevin. Then Waddlesworth stole the guard's keys and set Kevin and the others free!

With Fluffy's help, Chloe escaped from the fur room, and arrived at her apartment at the same time as Kevin.

"Something rotten in Denmark! Rotten in Denmark!" cawed Waddlesworth. Chloe's apartment was ransacked. Her dogs and their dognapper were gone.

Drooler found a train ticket that LePelt had dropped. "The Orient Express at ten!" cried Chloe.

Cruella and LePelt were standing outside the train
station examining the puppies LePelt had stolen.
Cruella picked up Oddball. Oddball was wearing a

spotted sweater, but she still did not have any spots of her own. "I asked for spotted dogs!" Cruella shrieked. "And you brought me a white rat!" She dropped Oddball.

51

The brave pup ran off to find her family.

Oddball found the right train. She raced alongside it as Kevin and Chloe arrived with the others.

Oh no! Oddball was in danger of falling onto the tracks! Waddlesworth flapped into the air, scooped up Oddball, and placed her safely on the train. "Dogs can fly!" he squawked.

Once in Paris, Cruella, Alonso, and LePelt drove to
LePelt's workshop. Alonso put the dogs into the cellar.
Waddlesworth and Oddball had been hiding in

Cruella's car. Now they sneaked into the workshop
and freed the puppies.

When Cruella caught sight of Oddball leading
the puppies out of the cellar, she dashed after them.
Oddball led the puppies into a bakery next door.

The bakery machine started up and . . .
slip–slide–splat! Cruella fell into a vat.
The pups pushed bags of flour into the vat.

Cruella tried, but she couldn't get out of the sticky batter.

Now it was time to bake a cake!

Kevin, Chloe, and Kevin's pets tracked the puppies
to the bakery. When they arrived, they saw that

Cruella was no match for one hundred and two Dalmatians.
The pups had baked her into a Cruella cake!

Kevin and Chloe celebrated with their pets. They found more good news waiting for them in London. The judge was sending Cruella back to prison—and donating her fortune to Second Chance.

And someone else received a special gift, too. There would be no more spotted sweaters for Oddball. She finally had the real thing!